RETURN TO THE
LIBRARY OF DOOM

BLOOD IN THE LIBRARY

BY MICHAEL DAHL

ILLUSTRATED BY
BRADFORD

www.raintreepublishers.co.uk
Visit our website to find out
more information about
Raintree books.

To order:
☎ Phone 0845 6044371
🖷 Fax +44 (0) 1865 312263
✉ Email myorders@raintreepublishers.co.uk

Customers from outside the UK please telephone +44 1865 312262

Raintree is an imprint of Capstone Global Library Limited, a company
incorporated in England and Wales having its registered office at 7 Pilgrim
Street, London, EC4V 6LB – Registered company number: 6695582

Text © Stone Arch Books 2012
First published in the United Kingdom in hardback and paperback by
Capstone Global Library Ltd in 2012
The moral rights of the proprietor have been asserted.

Art Director: Kay Fraser
Graphic Designer: Hilary Wacholz
Production Specialist: Michelle Biedscheid
Originated by Capstone Global Library Ltd
Printed in and bound in China by Leo Paper Products Ltd

ISBN 978 1 406 23697 2 (paperback)
15 14 13 12 11
10 9 8 7 6 5 4 3 2 1

British Library Cataloguing in Publication Data
A full catalogue record for this book is available from the British Library.

Contents

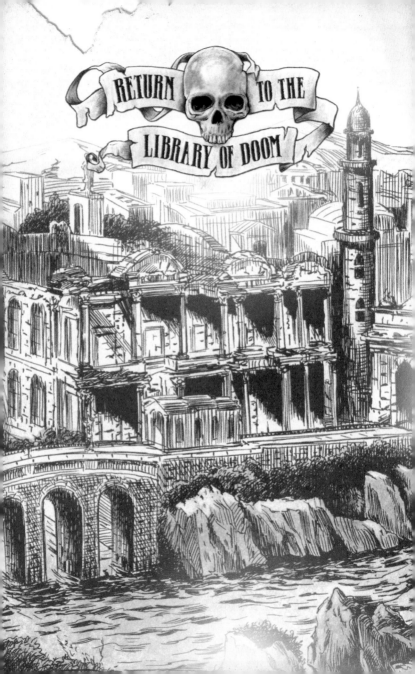

RETURN TO THE LIBRARY OF DOOM

Behold the Library of Doom! The world's largest collection of deadly and dangerous books. Only the Librarian can prevent these books from falling into the hands of those who would use them for evil.

BUT THE LIBRARIAN CAN'T LIVE FOREVER. OR CAN HE . . . ?

Chapter 1

HEARTBEAT

Deep within the Library of Doom, someone is bleeding.

A young man stands on a ladder. He stares at his hand.

Blood oozes from his finger. It **STAINS** his white glove.

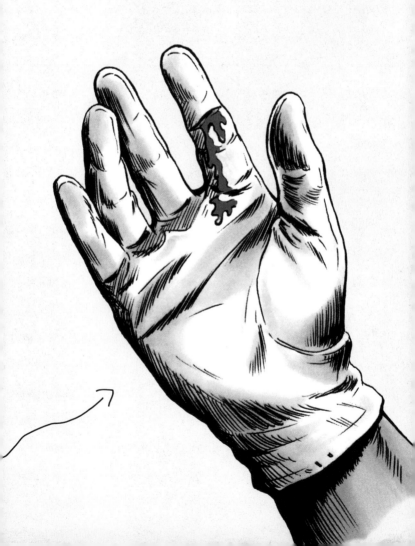

The young man is Alonso, one of the sub-librarians. He is working in one of the DEEPEST levels of the great library.

Alonso stares at his finger. "Stupid paper cut!" he says.

Alonso doesn't **remember** getting the paper cut, but he has been working with books all night.

He hears a sound that reminds him of a heartbeat.

DOOM ... DOOM ... DOOM ...

The sound throbs in his head.

The ladder **vibrates**.

Then Alonso hears the voices.

Chapter 2

THE ARCHIVISTS

Alonso quietly climbs **DOWN** his ladder.

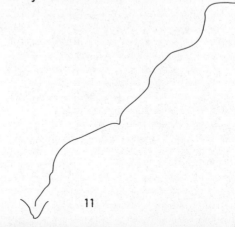

He follows the echoing voices down several dark hallways.

Soon, he comes to a window with metal bars.

Alonso PEERS down through the bars.

He sees shadows moving on the
floor of the room.

It is a CIRCLE of tall, thin men.

Alonso recognizes them. They are
the ARCHIVISTS.

Day and night, the Archivists
wander through the Library of Doom.

They **NEVER** sleep.

They **NEVER** eat.

They make sure that every book is in its place. If they notice a book missing, they report it to the Librarian.

The men are **arguing** with a young woman. She is Skywriter.

"He can't be gone!" shout**S** Skywriter.

"We have NOT heard from the Librarian in many months," says one of the TALL men.

Another Archivist nods his long, thin head. "Something is wrong," he says. "I fear it can mean only one thing. The Librarian is dead."

Chapter 3

FOE

Dead? Alonso feels a cold **CHILL** in his heart.

Then he hears the drumming again.

DOOM ... DOOM ... DOOM ...

The Archivists are still talking.

"The last we heard from the Librarian," says one, "he was heading towards the UNDER LIBRARY."

"Yes, yes," says another. "He heard that the Eraser is inside."

"The Eraser?" asks Skywriter.

Alonso knows that name. The Eraser is the Librarian's **deadliest** FOE.

An Archivist steps forward. "The Eraser is planning to **DESTROY** our oldest books," he says.

"But how could the Eraser break into the Library?" asks Skywriter.

Watching from the window, Alonso knows the answer to her question.

A voice seems to speak in his mind.

The Eraser slipped *in through a bookworm hole.*

The Archivists and Skywriter hear the gasp. They look up.

Alonso ducks down below the window.

"We have no time to lose," he hears Skywriter say. "We must enter the **Under Library** and find the Librarian."

"It is too late," says one of the TALL men.

"It is never too late," says Skywriter.

Alonso runs away from the window and down the DARK hall. He must save the Librarian.

Chapter 4

TRAVEL BOOK

The **Under Library** is far below the main rooms of the Library of Doom.

Its seven levels are buried beneath layers of burning rock.

I have to get there fast, Alonso tells himself. *But how?*

He doesn't have POWERS, like Skywriter and the Librarian do.

It could take him hours to reach the buried rooms of the Under Library.

Alonso runs down the hall. He sees a **HUGE** book in a corner.

"Of course!" he says aloud.

He runs over to the book. On its cover are the words *Short Stories*.

Alonso opens the **HEAVY** cover.

He sees a dark (hole.)

"This will take me there in no time," he says.

Then Alonso jumps into the hole.

Volumes of short stories are s^{c}att$_e$red throughout the huge Library.

The books shorten the stories that a person has to **travel** through.

The hole that Alonso is falling through passes through hundreds of levels in the main Library.

It reaches down to the Under Library.

In a few seconds, Alonso's feet hit the floor of a shadowy room.

He lands with a **thud**.

Oof!

His hands hit the stone floor.

He is on the first story of the Under Library.

Alonso looks at his finger.

It has stopped bleeding.

The blood reminds him of something.
But what?

He stands STILL and listens.

All he can hear is the **strange**
heartbeat sound.

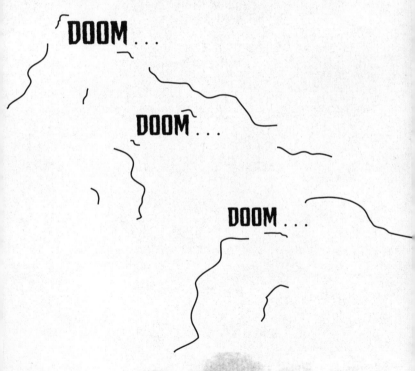

DOOM...

DOOM...

DOOM...

He sees a faint glow in the distance.

The heartbeat grows louder.

Alonso walks towards the light.

Chapter 5

THE ERASER

The light comes from a **GIANT** reading room.

Candles burn in iron chandeliers hanging from the ceiling.

Alonso sees Skywriter. She has her back to him.

She is facing a man with greenish skin and sad eyes.

The man has black hair that moves and flickers like a dark flame.

"You don't belong here, ERASER," says Skywriter.

Alonso hides and watches from the shadows.

He sees the man smile.

"You think you can **DEFEAT** me?" asks the man.

"You'll just end up like <u>he</u> did," the Eraser says.

The Eraser points to a TALL mound of books lying next to him.

Sticking out from the bottom of the pile is a gloved hand. Alonso recognizes the glove.

It belongs to the <u>Librarian</u>.

Skywriter rushes to the mound. She shoves the heavy books aside.

The body of the Librarian lies beneath them.

"Watch your fingers," says the Eraser. "Or you'll suffer the same **fate**."

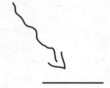

Fingers? wonders Alonso.

"What are you talking about?"
DEMANDS Skywriter.

The Eraser laughs. "The powerful
Librarian died from something oh so
small," he says. "A paper cut."

Suddenly, Alonso feels **sick** to his
stomach.

"That's impossible!" cries Skywriter.

"He's not breathing, is he?" says
the Eraser. The Eraser picks up one of
the books that had been lying on the
Librarian.

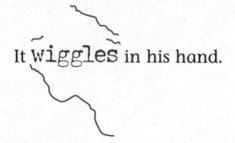

It wiggles in his hand.

"It was all part of my plan to get rid of him," says the Eraser. "I left a BOOK with steel edges lying open. I knew that the Librarian would want to look through it. Especially since I told him that it held the key to my plan. Which it did."

"As soon as he cut his finger, a drop of blood **oozed** out," says the Eraser. "These books smell blood from miles away. I placed a curse on them: Find the blood of the Librarian and attack! Attack until the heart stops beating!"

Still hidden in the shadows, Alonso feels as if a thousand insects are crawling on his skin.

His thoughts are confused.

Where . . . where am I? he wonders.

The sound in his ears grows louder.

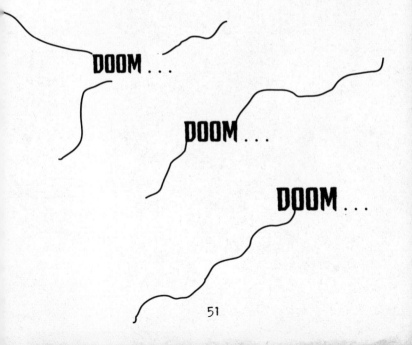

DOOM . . .

DOOM . . .

DOOM . . .

"My swarm of books found him. They sucked the life out of him," says the Eraser.

His strange black hair flickers angrily.

"And now, the LIBRARY OF DOOM is at my mercy."

Chapter 6

THE CURSE
AND THE CURE

"NEVER!" shouts Skywriter.

Raging fire blazes from her fingers

and shoots towards the Eraser.

The Eraser laughs. He RAISES his hands, and the flames disappear. "You'll need more than that to defeat me," he says.

"Then how's this!" Alonso shouts.

He steps forward, out of the (shadows.) He points his hand at the Eraser.

Golden flames burst from the finger that had been bleeding before.

Alonso's flames join those from Skywriter.

They twist together into a burning, flickering chain.

55

"The Librarian can **NEVER** be terminated," said Alonso. "He can never be fired. But you can!"

FLAMES surround the shrieking Eraser. "No!" he screams.

The Eraser is trapped within a fiery, gold cage.

Skywriter *glances* up at Alonso. "Who are you?" she asks.

Alonso **DROPS** to his knees, exhausted. "I'm a sub . . ." he begins.

"Substitute?" asks Skywriter.

Alonso looks up at her. His face brightens. He smiles. "Exactly," he says. "I'M A SUBSTITUTE."

Alonso looks at the body of the Librarian. *My body*, he thinks.

"The Eraser's curse said to find the blood and attack. His **book creatures** could only attack my body," Alonso says.

Skywriter stares at the young man. "What are you saying?" she asks.

"Nothing can **DESTROY** the heart of the Librarian," says Alonso. "If I had a new shape, I wouldn't be the Librarian anymore, would I? At least I wouldn't be the Librarian under the **CURSE**."

Skywriter stands up. "You mean," she says, "that you are –"

"The Librarian?" finishes Alonso. "Yes, that was my plan."

"After I cut my finger, I knew I couldn't outrun the Eraser's creatures," says Alonso. "My only way to escape was to become someone else. Someone that the Eraser would never suspect."

Suddenly, the body on the floor is gone.

LIGHT fills the room.

Skywriter *sees* the Librarian standing next to her.

"I can't believe that was YOU," she says.

The Librarian smiles. "Don't **judge** a book by its cover," he says.

AUTHOR

Michael Dahl is the author of more than 200 books for children and young adults. He has won the AEP Distinguished Achievement Award three times for his non-fiction. His Finnegan Zwake mystery series was shortlisted twice by the Anthony and Agatha awards. He has also written the Library of Doom series. He is a featured speaker at conferences on graphic novels and high-interest books for boys.

ILLUSTRATOR

Bradford Kendall has enjoyed drawing for as long as he can remember. As a boy, he loved to read comic books and watch old monster films. He graduated from university with a BFA in Illustration. He has owned his own commercial art business since 1983, and lives with his wife, Leigh, and their two children, Lily and Stephen. They also have a cat named Hansel and a dog named Gretel.

GLOSSARY

archivist someone whose job is to maintain archives or records

chandeliers decorative hanging light

fate what will happen to someone

foe an enemy

recognize see or hear someone and know who the person is

substitute someone who is a replacement for someone else

suffer experience something bad, hard, or painful

suspect have an idea that someone is guilty, but not have proof

vibrates shake very quickly

volume a book

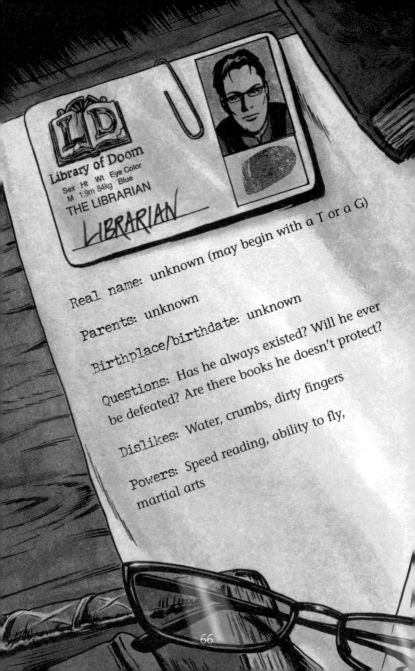

LD
Library of Doom
Sex Ht Wt Eye Color
M 1.9m 84kg Blue
THE LIBRARIAN

LIBRARIAN

Real name: unknown (may begin with a T or a G)

Parents: unknown

Birthplace/birthdate: unknown

Questions: Has he always existed? Will he ever be defeated? Are there books he doesn't protect?

Dislikes: Water, crumbs, dirty fingers

Powers: Speed reading, ability to fly, martial arts

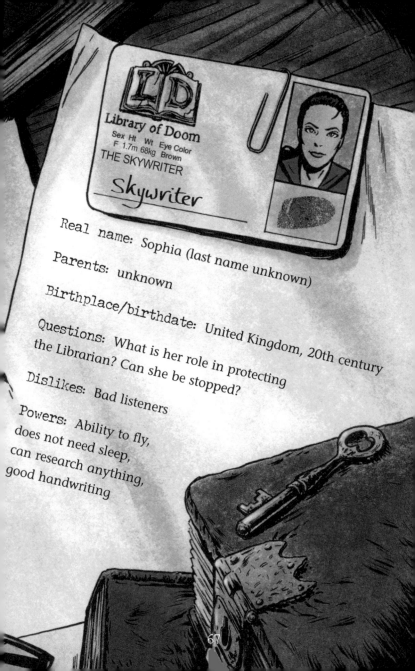

Library of Doom

Sex Ht   Wt   Eye Color
F   1.7m 68kg Brown

THE SKYWRITER

Skywriter

Real name: Sophia (last name unknown)

Parents: unknown

Birthplace/birthdate: United Kingdom, 20th century

Questions: What is her role in protecting the Librarian? Can she be stopped?

Dislikes: Bad listeners

Powers: Ability to fly, does not need sleep, can research anything, good handwriting

THE ERASER

The Eraser is one of the Librarian's oldest enemies. For centuries, the Eraser has sought to destroy that which the Librarian holds most dear: the books in the Library of Doom. In fact, the Eraser would like to destroy the Librarian himself.

So far, the Eraser has not been able to defeat the Librarian. Though the Librarian did lose four priceless old books to his enemy, he and Skyriter spent a year hunting for replacements. They have found new copies of three of the four books.

The Eraser is a threat, but not one the Librarian fears. At least not right now.

DISCUSSION QUESTIONS

1. Why did the Eraser want to **DESTROY** the Librarian?

2. **Alonso** was the Librarian's replacement. What do you think happened to the real Alonso? Explain your answer.

3. What questions do you still have about this story? Discuss them!

WRITING PROMPTS

1. Imagine that you are someone's SUBSTITUTE. Who would you want to be? Write about it.

2. It can be very interesting to think about a story from another person's point of view. Try writing this story, or part of it, from Skywriter's point of view. What does she SEE, HEAR, THINK, and SAY? What does she notice? How is the story different?

3. Create a **COVER** for a book. It can be this book or another book you like, or a made-up book. Don't forget to write the information on the back, and include the author and illustrator names!

More books from the Library of Doom

Return to the Library of Doom